The undersea world is a magical place for Dilo. Everywhere he goes there are surprising animals and plants to see and something new to discover. Then one day he meets a girl in the sea. Her name is Debra. It is the start of many new adventures.

Dilo's Early Days

Dilo was born in a quiet bay. Dilo's mother was alone when he first came into the undersea world. She taught him about the tides and the plants and animals. Dilo and his mother became good companions. In fact you could say they were best friends. Dilo was mischievous and curious. Sometimes his curiosity got him into trouble but his mother knew that was all part of growing up. She also knew that Dilo would want to roam. *The Call of the Deep* was what she called the urge to travel that they both had inside them.

When he was old enough Dilo and his mother set off on a long journey together. They had many experiences and adventures on the way. Then one day, after Dilo had been playing with a seal, Dilo's mother got caught in a net. Dolphin spirits came to carry her to the next world. Dilo wanted to go with them. But they told him he must stay. "You have a mission" they said. "That is why you have a star on your dorsal fin. But only those who know you have a mission will be able to see it."

When Dilo's mother died Dilo could still feel her presence. It was all around him. At night, when the sky was clear, he could see her outlined in the stars. He knew she would always be there to protect and comfort him.

The full story of Dilo's early life is told by Horace Dobbs in his book **Dilo and the Call of the Deep** illustrated by Rico, Watch Publishing ISBN 0 9522389 5 0.

Books by Horace Dobbs

CAMERA UNDERWATER

UNDERWATER SWIMMING

SNORKELLING AND SKINDIVING
AN INTRODUCTION

FOLLOW A WILD DOLPHIN

SAVE THE DOLPHINS

DOLPHIN SPOTTER'S HANDBOOK

THE MAGIC OF DOLPHINS

THE GREAT DIVING ADVENTURE

CLASSIC DIVES OF THE WORLD

TALE OF TWO DOLPHINS

DANCE TO A DOLPHIN'S SONG

JOURNEY INTO DOLPHIN DREAMTIME

DOLPHIN HEALING

The Dilo Collection

Dilo and the Call of the Deep

Dilo makes Friends

Dilo and the Treasure Hunters

Dilo and the Witch of Black Rock

Dilo's Fun and Activities Book

Fascinating Facts about Dolphins

Dilo's Adopt and Watch Handbook

Contents

Dilo's Early Days
Dedication

Page	Chapter	Title
9	1	The red star
14	2	Breakfast
21	3	Eyes in the sand
25	4	The kelp forest
29	5	Bad news
36	6	A good sign
43	7	Arrival
53	8	Porridge
58	9	Shark
63	10	Drug runners
68	11	Girl on a dolphin
77	12	A new world
84	13	"Help"
89	14	Rescue
94	15	In the news
100	16	Picnic on the cliffs
107	17	Sea Wolf
112	18	Twin propellers
119	19	A ray of hope
122	20	R & R
131	21	In peak condition
138		Notes
139		Picture. Request from the author
140		Letters from the author
142		International Dolphin Watch
143		Dolphin Shop. Dilo Dome

First published in 1995

Reprinted 2005

Watch Publishing
International Dolphin Watch
10 Melton Road
North Ferriby
East Yorkshire HU14 3ET
England
Tel: 01482 632650/645789
Fax: 01482 634914
Email: idw@talk21.com
www.idw.org

A catalogue record for this book is available
from the British Library

ISBN 0 9522389 2 6

Founded 1978

Printed by
Redcliff Print & Design
30 The Weir
Hessle
East Yorkshire
HU13 ORU
Tel: 01482 640428 Fax: 01482 641390

HORACE DOBBS

Makes Friends

Illustrations by
Rico

Dedication

This book is for *Fiona and Rebecca Parker* to celebrate the time we went out dolphin watching together from the little harbour of Findochty in the Moray Firth.

It is also dedicated to *Daisy and Kerri MacDonald* and the folks of Findochty who made our visit so memorable, enjoyable and exciting.

1 The red star

It was dark and still. There was no moon. Dilo the young dolphin was alone and a little afraid. He was moving silently through the black water. He rose, took a breath and slid back beneath the surface leaving barely a ripple - just as his mother taught him.

In the brief time Dilo was on the surface he saw the heavens speckled with stars. There was one that was quite different from the rest. He had not seen it before. It was red and the lowest in the sky. He was heading directly towards it. The salmon were swimming in the same direction. They were heading for a river to spawn in. Dilo hoped they would lead him to a place where he could feed easily - where there were rocks and gullies to hide and play in - where he could feel secure and grow to full size.

Dilo wished the dawn would come. He wouldn't feel so nervous if the sun was in the sky. He pretended his mother was by his side. She always knew when he needed comfort and reassurance and would stroke him gently with her flippers.

Dilo heard a sound. It was far off, faint as a heartbeat, but regular. He continued to swim steadily. Each time he surfaced he fixed on the red star. The sound was getting louder. Whatever was making the sound was also heading towards the red star. It could spell danger. Should he change course?

"If my mother was here she would know exactly what to do," Dilo told himself.

At last the sun came up and laid a path of shimmering orange light across the sea. The sky lightened and the stars faded - all except the red one - which was not a star at all. It was the light from a small lighthouse perched on top of the cliffs.

High above the land the seagulls, black against the pale grey sky, were scouting for food. They headed towards the source of the throbbing sound. They were in luck. A fishing boat was coming back into port. Onboard the fishermen were gutting their catch and throwing entrails over the side. The gulls swooped down and plucked up their breakfast from the water.

Miles away other gulls detected the diving birds. It was a sign that food was available. They headed towards the fishing boat. Soon the noise of the screeching birds following the trawler reached a crescendo.

Dilo couldn't resist the urge to join them. All of his fear evaporated. He bounded across the water as fast as he could towards the boat.

From underneath Dilo saw a piece of dead fish floating on the surface. He headed up towards it. But just as he reached the scrap of fish a seagull dropped out of the sky and snatched it away, it's sharp beak just missing the dolphin. Both the seagull and the dolphin were startled by their unexpected meeting.

The seagull gulped down the food as fast as it could, and immediately rose again, squawking loudly. Dilo decided that food scraps were not for him. Anyway, there was too much competition from the birds.

Dilo felt the water pulsing. It was the backwash from the propeller. He swam into the stream and enjoyed the invisible waves as they passed over his body. Soon he reached their source and was swimming with his nose, or beak, a short distance behind the propeller. The sensation was wonderful. His entire body was vibrating.

Moments later Dilo veered off and then swam towards the bow of the boat. Someone onboard spotted him. The fishermen stopped working. They moved to the side of the boat, and looked down into the water. The dolphin sped past the bright red hull. The sun dappled Dilo's dark grey body as it arrowed up through the water. The men waited for the dolphin to come up. Dilo obliged. The top of his head briefly touched the surface of the sea. His blowhole opened. The dolphin breathed with a noisy puff. The sun glistened on his wet, domed head. A cloud of spray was blown into the air and a rainbow glowed in it. Then the dolphin dived. The entire breathing cycle had taken less than a second, but it had left a more permanent image in the memories of the fishermen. Dilo raced on towards the front of the boat. There, with the ease and grace of an expert skier whizzing downhill, Dilo rode the bow wave - weaving this way and that ahead of the trawler.

2 Breakfast

The lighthouse keeper came out of his cottage to enjoy the dawn. He was proud of his light which guided the ships safely into the harbour.

There was a time when he polished the copper lamp until it shone like gold. Every night he would light the wick. And every morning he would turn it down until the flame went out. That was until the workmen came. They ran an electricity cable across the fields to the lighthouse. The oil lamp was changed to an electric light bulb which switched itself on and off automatically. So the keeper no longer had a job. He stayed-on in the lighthouse cottage because he liked watching seabirds and enjoyed seeing the ships pass by. But he knew one day he would have to leave.

The ex-lighthouse keeper puffed on his pipe and watched the fishing boat approach. When he spotted the dolphin cavorting in the bow wave the man felt a great inner joy. It reminded him of the days when he was at sea.

Somehow Dilo sensed the presence of the man on the top of the cliff. There was a connection between them - a bond that linked two free spirits. Lifting half his glistening body clear of the water the dolphin rose in front of the boat. For a moment Dilo resembled a ship's figurehead before slipping back down into the bow wave.

From his high perch the lighthouseman was better able to know what the dolphin was doing than the men on the deck of the trawler. They continued to peer over the side when the dolphin disappeared from view. The man on the cliffs

17

could see clearly what had happened. Dilo had taken-up a new position just behind the boat. His beak was close to the propeller. This alarmed the lighthouse keeper who knew the rotating blades of a bronze propeller could be as deadly as a circular saw.

The dolphin seemed to be tempting fate. Closer and closer he went until the tip of this beak was almost touching the swirling blades. In fact the dolphin was quite safe as long as he stayed behind them. After enjoying a vibro-massage Dilo fell back and let the boat move away. Then he accelerated forward at full speed, swam right around the hull, and leapt high out of the water. The knives of the fishermen glinted silver in the air as they waved their approval of Dilo's spectacular leap.

"Did you see that?" "Wow, what a jump." "Look at that," the fishermen shouted together.

The lighthouse keeper watched the fishing boat take the deep channel that led safely to the jetty. He wondered what the dolphin would do next. Dilo had disappeared. Then the man saw a fin rise briefly close to the far cliffs. Immediately after the dolphin submerged a circular pool of flat water, ringed with ripples, appeared on the surface. As an ex-fisherman he knew the dolphin was feeding.

With phenomenal acceleration the dolphin rushed forward and grabbed a salmon. The dolphin's teeth were clamped onto his prey. The luckless fish had no chance of escape. But Dilo was in a playful mood. He let the salmon escape and then caught it again.

When Dilo surfaced with the fish he sensed he was being watched. He could not resist showing off his trophy. The dolphin tossed the fish high out of the water, caught it and swallowed it head first. The watching man took the pipe from his mouth and waved the stem in the air. His movements were unhurried. Time was something he had plenty of.

A cat jumped up onto the wall and rubbed its head against the lighthouse keeper's face. A dog brushed past his legs. Having gained his master's attention it looked-up pleadingly.

"I know it's time for our breakfast too," said the man.

The animals followed him indoors where glowing embers of driftwood were heating a saucepan of water on an ancient kitchen range.

Both Dilo and the lighthouse keeper were aware that their lives were about to change. But neither knew what the future had in store.

3　Eyes in the sand

After swallowing the fish Dilo set out to explore his new home. The dolphin found himself in a bay that was flat and sandy like the one in which he was born. He decided to see if there were any of the shellfish he remembered. His mother told him they were scallops, but he called them Clop-Clops because when they swam their shells went "Clop,Clop".

His sonar picked up something ahead hiding in the sand. It wasn't a Clop-Clop. He moved forward so he could see it both with his eyes as well as his magic sound. As he got close he saw what looked like two tiny stones side by side. But his sound told him they were not made of stone. Closer and closer he went.

They swivelled slightly.

They were eyes.

"But you don't just see two eyes sitting on the sand all by themselves," Dilo said to himself. "I know what you are."

The dolphin inched forward until the tip of his beak was almost touching them.

At that instant there was a flurry in the sand. A flatfish, which had buried itself with just its eyes showing, rose off the bottom. It shook the sand off its body and fluttered across the seabed like a newspaper blown across a street. Dilo followed behind in pursuit. The frightened plaice quickly became exhausted and flopped down onto the gravel. In an instant its colour changed. It became covered with spots that matched the stones and sand around it.

The fish stayed perfectly still hoping that the dolphin wouldn't see through its new disguise. Dilo did of course, but continued on his way thinking the fish would make a tasty snack if he got hungry.

"What a strange creature," the dolphin mused to himself. "Fancy having both eyes on the same side of your body."

As he swam along he noticed several more pairs of eyes. They all belonged to fish that were as flat as pancakes.

"I suppose it is sensible to have both eyes on the top of your head if you spend most of your time on the flat sea bed."

Dilo continued his exploration, flying over

the sandy sea bed with gentle up and down movements of his tail.

He came to an area covered with lots of little pyramids. They looked as if they had been made by someone squirting out the whole of a tube of toothpaste filled with sand. Dilo knew the mounds were pushed up by worms burrowing under the surface. His mother had told him about the 'Undersand World'.

A little swimming crab panicked when it saw Dilo's dark shape suddenly appear overhead. It raced sideways over the sand and then decided the safest thing to do was to disappear. It stopped. With its legs flailing the crab quickly scooped out a hollow in the sand, pulled itself backwards into it, and disappeared. Although Dilo couldn't see it with his eyes he knew exactly where the crab was because he was also scanning the bottom with his sonar.

4 The kelp forest

Dilo continued to explore his new territory. He swam out of the bay through the channel towards the open sea. Using his long distance sound he saw a shoal of mackerel sweeping through water like a fast moving cloud. They were whirling around a large rock that rose out of the seabed right up to the surface. To Dilo it was like a mountain rising out of a flat sandy plain.

Dilo swam to investigate. When he got closer he saw that the rock was rich with sea life - like a garden. There were starfish, sea urchins and anemones that looked like flowers. Near the surface was a forest of kelp. Dilo nosed into it - he was a very inquisitive dolphin. Under the thick green canopy the rocks were completely covered with encrustations of many pale hues - mostly pink and cream. Clinging to the rocks were crabs. Some with long spidery legs had little bits of seaweed stuck to their spiky red-brown shells. Others - less colourful - were smooth. They squatted on the rocks and held their powerful claws close to their bodies until Dilo got close. Then they raised them menacingly.

Dilo continued to explore the kelp forest. It was very mysterious. Then he found two long feelers poking out of a crevice. He peered in. In the dark shadow he could see two eyes looking at him. As Dilo approached the occupant moved forward waving two huge claws. The dolphin backed away. He knew from experience they could give him a very nasty nip.

"Good morning Mister Lobster," he said cheerfully, keeping well out of biting range.

"Nice day isn't it?"

Dilo moved on. He didn't wait for an answer. He had already concluded it really was a nice day and decided to stay in the area for a time. There was plenty of food and lots of places to explore.

He rose to the surface and hovered quietly looking with his eyes. He was in a huge bay. In one direction was the open sea. The rock he had been exploring rose out of the water. In the far distance were ranges of misty mountains. Close by were high cliffs. Many were splashed with white bird droppings. On the ledges he could see nesting gulls. Above them the sky was filled with wheeling wings. Raucous squawks floated through the clear air.

On one cliff top the white-washed finger of the lighthouse was bathed in sunlight. Next to it stood the square block of a house with a grey, slate roof. The lighthouse keeper was outside enjoying the sun sparkling on the deep blue sea. A postman was walking along the cliff-top path towards the lighthouse. A dog ran out of the cottage barking furiously.

5 Bad News

The postman was what you would call a philosophical man. He had been to university and had once run a factory. Then he decided he didn't want that kind of job in a city anymore. So he became a postman in a little fishing village and never regretted the change. He liked taking letters to the isolated lighthouse. He would leave his van in the beach car park and walk up the long cliff path. The postman kept the letters for the lighthouse until the end of his round. Then he could spend time talking to the keeper. He took with him a bottle of fresh milk and a packet of digestive biscuits to share over a cup of tea.

The lighthouse keeper who had little formal education was also a philosophical man. He looked forward to his visits from the postman especially in the winter when few people walked along the cliff top path. They would sit on opposite sides of the range. The lighthouse keeper would light up his pipe. If the weather was really cold he would pour a tot of grog into the tea. This was stirred in after adding two generous teaspoons of sugar taken from an ancient tin labelled TEA that was kept on the mantleshelf over the range.

"Good morning Postie," said the lighthouse keeper. "What have you got for me to-day?"

"I've brought you the usual," the postman replied handing over the bottle of milk and a packet of digestive biscuits. "I've also got these. This one looks official," he continued, looking at one of the letters. "But this one is handwritten," he said before handing the lighthouseman two letters.

The dog stopped barking and was wagging his tail. Then he jumped up and put his paws on the postman's middle.

"Get down Boka," ordered the lighthouse keeper. "Come in." The two men walked through into the kitchen followed by the dog who was rushing around excitedly.

The fire in the range glowed orange in the dim light. On top a black kettle with a long spout, curved like a swan's neck, was singing gently. The lighthouse keeper took a packet of tea from beside the sugar tin. He emptied some tea into his cupped hand and transferred half a handful into a dark brown teapot he kept warm beside the stove. He took the teapot to the kettle. He didn't lift the heavy kettle. He just tilted it. The water poured out smoothly from the tall spout straight into the dark-stained interior of the teapot.

"I saw a dolphin in the bay this morning," he said as he put the teapot onto a plain wooden table. On it a ginger cat sat like one of the lions in Trafalgar Square. The cat, called Sprat, barely moving, looked disdainfully at the dog who was still rushing around as if he had a firework tied to his tail.

The lighthouseman took a couple of cups and a tin from the dresser. The biscuit tin, like everything else around him, was well-worn. The lid was decorated with a crazed, old-fashioned picture of a king and queen. Curved over their heads was the word CORONATION in dull gold letters.

The lighthouse keeper stirred the tea inside the teapot. He filled a saucer of milk and placed it on the table in front of the cat. Then, taking a tea strainer from the wooden drawer at the end of the table, he poured out two mugs of tea.

The two men pulled up their chairs to opposite sides of the table.

"Now let's see what news you've brought for me. I'll start with this one," said the keeper, opening the letter with the typed address.

He read it silently to himself. A look of dismay crossed his face. The postman could see it wasn't good news.

"What does it say?" he enquired.

"Dear Sir," said the lighthouseman after a pause, "now that you are no longer in our employ you are not entitled to occupy the lighthouse cottage. As you know the cottage was severely damaged during the winter gales and we carried out temporary repairs to the roof. We cannot justify the cost of bringing the cottage to the new standards required for permanent habitation. We regret therefore that we must ask you to vacate the premises within three months. Yours faithfully, E. J. Henderson. Supervisor."

The postman looked sympathetically at his

companion.

"That is the thing I have feared most since they made me redundant," said the lighthouseman after a pause. "I love it here and was hoping they would let me stay on."

"I suppose that's the price of progress," commented the postman. "What will you do?"

"I don't know," said the lighthouse keeper still looking bewildered. "I'm getting too old to go back on the boats as a deckhand. That's a job for a young man. Anyway the fishing's bad these days. I really don't know what to do."

"Perhaps the other letter's got better news," said the postman as cheerfully as he could. He recognised the writing. "I know, I bet it is from that young half sister of yours writing to say she's won the pools." He knew Mary was one of the few people who wrote to the lighthouse keeper.

"Some hope," said the other man still looking glum. He opened the letter with his thumb and read it out loud.

"Dear Patrick, I'm afraid I've got some bad news. I have to go into hospital for an urgent operation. The consultant said it will be touch and go for me. I don't know what's best for the twins. When I told them they would have to be put in care they cried. They said they would rather do anything than go into a home.

Robin said he has always wanted to come and stay with you. Debbie said she didn't want to be separated from her brother. They both said they would always be on their very best behaviour.

Their summer holidays start tomorrow and I have to go into hospital on Thursday. You haven't got a phone so I couldn't phone you. I had to make a decision. So I have told them they can come. They will be arriving at the railway station at 12.30 on Wednesday. If you meet them it will give you plenty of time to get back to light the lighthouse lamp. You are the only one I can turn to for help. Please, please don't be angry with me. I am at my wits end. Your loving sister, Mary."

6 A good sign

Pat and Postie were silent. Neither knew what to say to the other.

The ginger cat walked across the table and brushed himself against the arms of the lighthouse keeper who had his elbows on the table and was holding his mug of tea in both hands which were shaking slightly.

"What can I do?" said the lighthouse keeper at last. "I'm a bachelor. I've got my animals. I like living alone." He paused as if plucking up courage to say what was on his mind. Then he blurted it out. "The last thing I want is a couple of kids rushing around the place. They can't come here."

"Mary obviously doesn't know that the lighthouse has been automated and you've lost your job," said the postman eventually.

"And that I've got to leave my cottage," added the keeper.

"Sounds like things are even worse for her than they are for you."

"I know. That makes me feel bad."

The postman remembered the news in the letter he had brought from Mary the previous year.

"Her husband's left her. She's been bringing up the children on her own. Now she's got to go into hospital. She wouldn't ask for help unless it was really serious Pat. Things are obviously pretty desperate for Mary now," said the postman. "Seems like you are the only person she can turn to for help."

The lighthouse keeper went silent, staring straight ahead.

"I remember when Mary was born," he said eventually. "When my mother died my father married again - this young woman. I never got on with her. When they had Mary I left home. Went on the road. Worked here and there. Eventually ended up on the fishing boats. Never saw my father again. When I got the job of keeper I thought I'd stay put for a while. Now I've got to be on the move again."

He paused.

The postman kept silent.

"I haven't seen Mary for years. I've only seen the twins once. It was ages ago at their Christening. They were only babies then."

The postman could sense the battle going on inside the man sitting opposite him who was absent-mindedly stroking the cat. The dog had settled into the old armchair beside the fire. It sat there with its head on its front paws watching the two men intently. Boka's mind was firmly fixed on the biscuit tin.

"You've got to get out of the house soon. So why don't you give it a try? It's not as if Mary has asked you to look after her children for ever."

He could sense that the keeper was beginning to change his mind.

"It's summer. They can spend most of their time out of doors."

"I suppose you're right," the lighthouse keeper said at last. "But I still don't like the idea of having those children here."

The postman remembered Mary's previous letter. She said the children were so mischievous that the neighbours had called them "The Terrible Twins". He decided it was best not to mention this. He also felt the place needed a woman's touch if two children were to come and stay.

39

"How about my missus coming and helping you get this place sorted out a bit before they come?"

As soon as he had said it the postman realised he was on delicate ground. He remembered that several women had offered to come and tidy-up for his friend. But the lighthouse keeper always sent them on their way, later confiding with his postman friend, "I can't stand women fussing about the place."

So the postman made another suggestion.

"I'll tell you what. If the children get too much for you they can come round with me when I'm doing my deliveries."

"Alright," the keeper said reluctantly. "I'll give it a trial for a few days. But if they don't behave I'll send them packing. You see if I won't."

"I'm sure you won't regret it," said the postman. "Isn't it time we opened the biscuits?"

It was the moment Boka, the dog, had been waiting for. As soon as the lighthouse keeper picked up the packet the dog barked and thumped his tail against the back of the chair.

The lighthouseman gave the dog a biscuit before offering the packet to the postman. Then he took one himself and emptied the remainder into the Coronation tin.

The two men had a great love and understanding of one another. The postman always knew when it was time to leave. When he did they would go outside together and look out over the sea.

They followed the same routine the day the

two letters bearing bad news arrived. Just as they were about to go their separate ways the postman said, "I have a philosophy of life." He paused. "It is that every set-back is a stepping stone to something better."

"I'd like to believe you're right," said the lighthouse keeper.

As the men were stood together looking across the water Dilo the dolphin was completing his survey of the bay. He hadn't felt so happy for a long time. His joy built up like a clockwork spring. Then something inside triggered its release. He rushed up to the surface and jumped as high as he could five times in quick succession. It was a spectacular display. The two men on the cliff watched each silver arch as it formed and cascaded back into the sea. Their spirits rose instantly.

"That's a good sign," said the postman, his face lighting-up with delight. "Everything will turn out fine. You see if I'm not right!"

7 Arrival

Robin slipped in the mud. He tried to stop himself. The case he was carrying flew out of his hand and he fell headlong. He pulled himself up onto all fours, like a dog, and stayed like that for a few moments. He stood up unsteadily. Then his feet slid from under him and he fell back onto his bottom. Sitting on the ground Robin pushed his spectacles back into position, his hand covered with mud. The sky was grey and the rain was coming down in a steady drizzle. He could feel water oozing down his neck. He was not happy.

Debra who was ahead on the footpath turned round when her twin brother cried out. When she saw him, covered with mud, sitting in a dirty brown puddle, Debra burst out laughing.

"I suppose you think that's funny," growled

Robin indignantly.

"Yes I do," said Debra still shaking with uncontrollable mirth.

The lighthouse keeper was ahead of both of them, leading his nephew and niece across the fields towards his cottage. He was already regretting his decision to look after them. When he turned and saw the boy sitting in the mud he was furious at the lad's incompetence.

The ex-lighthouse keeper carefully propped against a stone wall the two heavy bags of groceries he was carrying. Then he picked his way along the track, his wellingtons squelching in the slimy ooze. He picked up the suitcase Robin had been carrying which was smeared with grey-brown clay.

"What have you got in here?" he asked, surprised at how heavy it was.

"I've got my computer and some books," said Robin. "And my clothes," he added as an afterthought.

"What on earth do you want a computer for?"

"For lots of things," he replied aggressively, feeling angry with himself for falling down.

"You and your computer," said Debra still laughing. Debra's laughter was infectious.

"You do look a sorry sight," said the lighthouse keeper beginning to see the funny side of the situation, but trying to remain serious.

"Here, give me your hand."

Robin held up a hand covered in brown, slimy mud.

"What a mess," said the lighthouse keeper pretending he was disgusted.

"You'll have to have a bath when we get to the lighthouse," said Debra.

"What bath?" injected the keeper. "All my water comes off the roof. I can't waste it on baths. But I may be able to spare a bowl-full to get you cleaned-up. You're not going to a hotel you know."

"Robin wipe your hands on the grass," suggested his sister.

Robin looked up at the grey, cloud-covered sky. All around everything was dripping. He felt like saying something about how ridiculous it seemed to him to talk about rationing water. Instead he said, "Have we got much further to go?"

As soon as he had uttered the words Robin

realised it wasn't a very intelligent question. He could clearly see the top of the lighthouse two fields away.

When Robin had wiped his hands he pulled up a tuft of grass and tried to wipe the mud off his clothes. But it only made the mess much worse.

"Don't do that, stupid," said Debra. "You can brush it off when it dries."

"That's if it ever stops raining," replied Robin disconsolately.

"Come on, let's get moving," said their uncle when his two charges had sorted themselves out. He led the way after he had picked up the two plastic bags whose handles were stretching to breaking point. As they climbed over a stone stile into the last field Boka came bounding across the grass barking loudly. The dog was obviously pleased to see his master. Boka's tail was wagging from side to side like a vibrating spring. He jumped up putting his muddy paws on the lighthouse man's dark yellow oil skins.

"Get down you stupid dog," commanded his owner. But Boka took no notice of the order - he was far too excited.

"Get down Boka," shouted the lighthouse keeper. Eventually Boka obeyed and rushed in a circle round the group at full speed before jumping up on Robin. Robin put down his suitcase and rubbed the dog's wet fur with his muddy hand - which conveniently cleaned it up a bit.

At last they reached the cottage. The keeper pushed open the unlocked door and the two youngsters followed him straight into the kitchen.

"Get those wet clothes off," he said,

removing his oil skins that were dripping pools of muddy water onto the flagstone floor. "We'll put them in the outhouse. Make yourself at home."

The children did as they were told and bundled their sopping coats onto their uncle's outstretched arm. When he went out across the small yard they looked at one another in wide-eyed wonder. They didn't have to speak their thoughts. Each knew what the other was thinking.

A few moments later their uncle returned with an armful of wood. He opened the iron doors of the range. Inside a tiny spot glowed red in the white ash. He removed the lid with a hooked iron bar and dropped some twigs onto the fire. In a few moments they crackled into flame.

"Robin, fill the kettle," he said, handing his nephew the big black kettle.

"There's a tap just by the back door."

Robin went outside to a large rectangular tank made from huge flat slabs of slate. Water running off the roof was gurgling into it from a

49

piece of plastic drain pipe held up with wire. At the bottom of the reservoir was a big brass tap. Gripping it with both hands Robin turned the stout handle. Water gushed out. When the kettle was full it was so heavy Robin had to carry it with both hands.

The fire was roaring.

"While the kettle's boiling I'll show you your room. Then we'll get something to eat."

The lighthouse keeper led the two bewildered children along a short dark passage. He turned a wobbly, ball-shaped brass handle in a brown door which creaked when he pushed it open.

The room the two children were shown into had a musty smell. There were two iron beds. The cast iron railings at each end were painted black. Some were capped with dull brass balls coated with varnish that had crazed and turned brown - like an old painting. The spring bases of the beds were made of thin wire that looked as if it had been loosely knitted into shape - like a pullover. It was red with rust in places but was nice and bouncy.

By the door a strip of newly installed brilliant-white insulating wire ran from the ceiling to a bright white switch that was screwed to the grey wall. The lighthouse keeper had switched it on when he entered the room. The bare light bulb hanging from a white cable in the centre of the ceiling lit everything with a dim yellow light.

In the centre of the creaking floorboards was a threadbare carpet. Its original flower design was just discernable. The wooden window frame was rotting and a thin film of water spread across the tiled windowsill. The window panes were spattered with raindrops. Some of them trickled downwards in jerky spurts as more were added. Through the window a low stone wall could be seen. Beyond that, just visible through the rain, was the heaving sea, grey and surly. The children looked out. They didn't know that under the waves there roamed a lonely dolphin.

8 Porridge

When the twins awoke the next day the sun was shining out of a clear sky. Through the cobwebbed window they could see the sea, turquoise blue, being gently rippled by a tiny breeze. They were soon up and dressed. In the kitchen three bowls were laid on the bare wooden table. A saucepan of thick porridge was standing on the range.

"Good morning Uncle Pat," said the children politely.

"Morning Robin. Morning Debbie. I trust you slept well."

"Yes thank you Uncle Pat."

"I hope you both like porridge."

The lighthouse keeper didn't wait for a reply and Robin didn't mention that porridge was definitely not one of his favourite breakfast cereals.

"Debbie will you fetch the milk. It's in a cooler under the water tank."

Debbie went outside. Under the bricks supporting the water tank was a chipped white enamel bowl half-filled with water. In it were two bottles of milk. Debbie took out one and handed it to her uncle who put it down on the table. The water running down the outside formed a dark circle where it stood .

The lighthouseman put three large heavy mugs on the table, a bowl of sugar, a tin of golden syrup, one saucer, three dessert spoons and finally the teapot. He told his niece and nephew to pull up two battered chairs and sit down on opposite sides of the table. He gave the porridge a vigorous stir with a large wooden spoon before dolloping it out into the bowls. Then he pressed the silver top of the milk bottle with his thumb. Removing the cap he carefully poured the first portion into the saucer. He then dispensed the remainder of the cream onto the three bowls of porridge.

"Come on Sprat," he called. The ginger cat, which had fled when the two children arrived, came out of its master's bedroom where it had spent the night on the bed. With a little coaxing the lighthouseman persuaded the cat to join them for breakfast. Sprat jumped up onto the table and squatted, nervously lapping the cream. The lighthouseman then levered open the top of the syrup tin with the end of a dessert spoon. He dipped one spoon after another into the tin and added a golden ball of syrup to each plate of porridge. Robin watched it melt and slowly flow into the creamy milk. Cats were discouraged from sleeping on beds and were *never* allowed on the table at home. He was very hungry and stared at the bowl in front of him. After a few mouthfuls Robin decided that porridge with milk and syrup was really rather good.

When they had finished breakfast Debra

said she wanted to go for a swim. She put on her costume. She and her brother got ready to descend the steps just beyond the wall. Robin, who couldn't swim and didn't like the water, decided he should go with his sister to the water's edge. He would have preferred to have stayed on the top of the cliffs with his nose in a book. He wasn't very good with heights either.

"Stay close to the rocks," instructed Debra's uncle before she left. "The current runs like a train further out at mid-tide. I'll watch you from up here. It's slack water at present."

He kept a dinghy attached to a running line off the bottom of the steps during the summer months. The twins looked down at the white clinker rowing boat moored offshore. Robin quickly worked out that it had to be kept well away from the land otherwise it would have grounded on the rocks when the tide fell.

"If you get tired swim to the dinghy rope and hold on till I pull you in," advised Uncle Pat.

The two youngsters picked their way cautiously down the uneven steps. At the bottom Debra removed the towel she had draped around her shoulders and gave it to her brother. She sat down on the bottom step and lowered her legs slowly into the sea.

"Oh!" she said as the cold took her breath away. Then she launched herself into the gulley and swam with strong breast strokes away from the land.

9 Shark

In the middle of the channel Dilo was cruising slowly over the seabed. Without thinking about it he was listening to the sounds all around him. They were part of his world. When Debra entered the water and started swimming he immediately became conscious of her presence although he couldn't see her. He focused his sonar on the new object. The echo that came back told him it was about the same size as a seal. But it was definitely not a seal. It wasn't moving very fast - so he could ignore it. But it was in the area that he had decided to live in - for the time being at least. So he decided to investigate. He had been taught how to do that by his mother. "Use your sonar, approach slowly and always from behind," she had instructed.

As he got closer his magic sound told him that the strange creature was a mammal because it had two air sacs in its chest. It had two tails and two flippers, all being waved at the same time. It appeared that the creature was using them for propulsion but they were very inefficient. There was a head and flowing back from it were long threads of hair. It was very unusual. He surfaced silently and decided it was safe enough to do a complete circle around the clumsy creature. Slowly he tightened the circle until the creature came into vision.

Through the blue green haze the dolphin could see Debra's arms and legs moving in unison as she continued to swim with the breast stroke. He decided that she posed no threat. Dilo was intrigued. So he moved in for a close inspection, surfacing just beside her and breathing in and out with a quick "ffouff".

The sound caused Debra to turn sideways. In that instant she saw a triangular fin very close. Shark. Terror pulsed through her like an electric shock. She didn't think for a fraction of a second. She panicked, screamed, and swam as fast as she could using overarm strokes. She saw Robin standing on the steps and headed towards him, hoping the monster would not get her before she reached safety. With arms flailing as fast as she could she snatched quick breaths.

Dilo was surprised by the sudden change in the strange creature. He sensed Debra's fear. The dolphin dived and headed out into the main channel.

When she got to the steps Debra hauled herself out and threw herself into the arms of her brother.

"Robin a shark came to get me," she cried between gasps of breath. "I've never been so frightened in all my life."

Robin held his sister and tried to calm her down.

"It's alright, you're safe now."

"Oh Robin I was so scared," sobbed Debra.

The lighthouse keeper, who had watched the whole incident, scrambled down the steps as quickly as he could. He reached the children a few moments after Debra climbed out of the sea.

'Oh Uncle Pat, did you see it - the shark - it was enormous - I thought it was going to eat me," Debra blurted out between sobs.

"It wasn't a shark."

"It was I saw it."

"It was a dolphin."

"A dolphin?" said Debra disbelievingly.

"You've made me all wet," said Robin realising his sister's panic was a false alarm.

"What a let down," he continued "I've never seen a shark."

"Oh don't be so beastly Robin. You wouldn't like it if I was bitten in half would you?" Debra cried indignantly.

10 Drug runners

Under the sea Dilo the dolphin heard another sound. A high pitched whine. He sank to the safety of the sandy seabed and turned on his sonar scan again. A strange object was coming towards him. It was staying on the surface and approaching fast, churning lots of air into the water. Soon it would be overhead. The water was very clear. He could see the surface. Then it appeared. A soft pointed nose, short body and a propeller at the back spinning round at a tremendous speed. In a flash it skimmed overhead and disappeared from view leaving a trail of bubbles that slowly dispersed. It was heading towards the rocks where he had just seen the slow strange creature that he knew he had frightened.

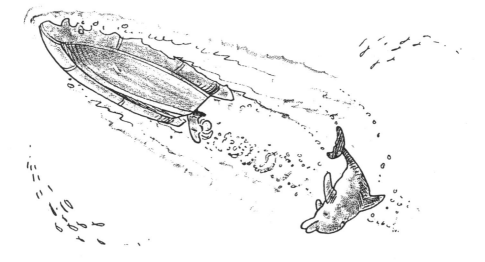

Robin and Debra also heard the sound. Looking into the bay they saw an inflatable. Spray was flying from the bows. It thundered across the sea. It was heading straight towards them and getting closer by the second.

"It's Mike," said their uncle. "I wonder what he wants?"

A few moments later the orange-red boat was rushing towards the rocks. Robin thought it would crash it was going so fast. But a short distance off Mike throttled back. The noise of the engines dropped to a quiet chatter. The boat slowed instantly. By the time it reached the rocks it was barely moving. Just as it got near the stern wave it had created reached it and pushed it forward. The soft rubber front bumped against the bottom step. Mike threw a rope to the lighthouseman who was waiting to catch it. He expertly tied it to a heavy iron ring hanging from a pin cemented into the rocks.

"And who have we here?" enquired Mike looking at the two children.

"They've come to stay for a while," replied the lighthouse keeper.

"My sister has just had a bit of a shock," chipped in Robin. "She thought she saw a shark, but it was only a dolphin."

"Only a dolphin," said Mike emphasising the word 'only'. He was wearing a red diving suit with black rubber seals round the neck and wrists.

"Are you coming up to the house?" asked the lighthouseman.

"No I can't stop. I've come across to let you

know that I have had a visit from the Customs men. They say they've heard there are drug runners in the area, and they've asked me to keep my eyes open for any suspicious boats. You've got the best look-out in the whole area so I thought I'd let you know."

"Can I help you Uncle Pat? I can record every boat that passes by on my computer," said Robin.

"That's a splendid idea," said Mike. "If you are going to do that I've got something back on *Merlin* that will be useful."

He turned to Debra and looked her up and down. "And seeing as you are obviously a swimmer I've got something for you too," he added. "I'll bring them over tomorrow morning."

With that Mike untied the rope and jumped nimbly into his inflatable boat. He yanked the starting cord. The engine throttled into life. It juddered as he backed slowly away. Mike put the engine into neutral, then into forward, and opened up the throttle. The boat responded instantly. It shot forward and curved in a graceful arc until it was pointing out to sea. Then it sped straight towards a large boat anchored in the bay.

"That's *Merlin*," said the lighthouseman, pointing towards the vessel. "It's a fully equipped diving ship. Mike's a good man. He runs it."

"What's this computer you're going on about?" he asked Robin as they climbed up the steps together.

11 Girl on a dolphin

That evening Robin emptied out the contents of his suitcase and spread them on the kitchen table. There were books on dinosaurs, birds, sharks and other creatures. He picked up *The Magic of Dolphins*, thumbed through it and handed the opened book to his sister.

"There, I told you dolphins weren't dangerous," he said. "Look, here's a picture of some children with wild dolphins."

Debra looked at it.

"Yes, but they are friendly dolphins."

"Well perhaps the one you saw today is a friendly dolphin," replied her brother.

"Do you think it is Uncle Pat?"

"Well it looked friendly enough when I saw it jumping around a fishing boat the other day."

The possibility that the dolphin who had frightened her could be friendly intrigued Debra. Just before she came away she had had a vivid dream about a dolphin. She had always liked dolphins. She even had several dolphin ornaments in her bedroom at home, but had left them all behind. Debra took the book away to the bedroom to read it quietly on her own.

Meanwhile her brother set up his computer.

"I've been recording the birds and the animals I've seen in a park close to our house," he said. He tapped a few keys. A map of the park came up on the screen. He tapped a few more keys and a picture of a goose appeared beside the pond. Robin changed the display.

"And here are the times and dates I saw them," he said to his uncle.

The lighthouse keeper was fascinated.

"I saw a fox one evening," Robin continued, and immediately brought the picture of a fox and all the details on the screen. He pushed a button and out popped a small square of plastic. Robin handed it to his uncle. "I store all the information on this. It's called a floppy disc. Then I post it off to International Wildlife Watch. They transfer the information to their data bank and send the floppy disc back to me."

He rummaged around to find a magazine.

"Here are some of the projects they do."

Robin thumbed through the pages.

70

"Look, here's one on seals - that should interest you," he said handing the magazine to his uncle. The lighthouseman skimmed through the article. Underneath it was a small advertisement captioned: *Warden Wanted.* After looking at the rest of the magazine he put it on the table.

Stepping across the room Robin's uncle took a book from the dresser. It was one of his few treasured possessions. The dust cover was torn and had bits missing. The book was well thumbed. It was a guide to seabirds. He handed it to his nephew.

"This is my special interest," he said. "Seabirds."

Robin was surprised to learn that his uncle knew the common names and the Latin names of all of the birds in the area of the lighthouse, and knew about their migrations. Both were happy to discover they had a common interest in wildlife and were pleased to share their knowledge and enthusiasm with one another. It was quite late before Robin closed-down his computer and went to bed.

The next morning Robin and Debra were leaning on the wall looking out to sea at the big dive boat in the bay. As they watched they saw the winch on the stern lowering an inflatable into the water. A few moments later it was skimming across the water towards them.

"Uncle Pat," yelled Debra to her uncle, "Mike's coming."

The lighthouse keeper arrived beside her with Boka barking loudly and rushing all over the place as usual.

"Look!" she screamed. "He's got the dolphin with him."

Sure enough, jumping in high loops behind the inflatable was Dilo - his body glistening with silver in the bright sunlight. Michael slowed down a little and did a huge circle in the bay. The dolphin responded immediately with another series of leaps.

From their position on the top of the cliffs
the three had a perfect view of the spectacular
display. Debra felt Dilo put on the show
especially for her benefit. So too did each of the
others. All three climbed down the steps. Just as
they reached the bottom the inflatable skimmed up
to the rocks. Mike stepped ashore to an excited
reception party.

"Look at me," he said. "I"m soaked from
head to foot."

"Good job you were wearing your diving suit," said Debra. The twins, Debra especially, were dying to know what he had brought for them. Mike saw her looking into the inflatable.

"It wouldn't matter if what I've brought you gets wet," he said to Debra, "but yours would," he said turning to Robin.

"Don't be a tease Mike," said Debra noticing him wink at her uncle. "What have you got for us?"

"Guess."

"No, I can't possibly."

"Alright then," said Mike jumping back into the inflatable and dipping into a bag. From it he pulled-out a snorkel and a pair of fins. Then he dug down and produced a wetsuit.

"This used to belong to my daughter but she's too big for it now," he said holding it up by the shoulders. "But it looks just right for you. Try it on."

Debra stepped into the legs, pushed her arms through the sleeves and Mike zipped-up the front.

"Perfect fit. It will keep you warm, stop you getting scratched on the rocks, and will act as a life jacket."

Debra wriggled with delight. She put on the fins which slapped on the rocks when she walked around. Then she pulled the mask into position.

"You look like a frog in spectacles," said Robin to his twin sister.

Mike jumped back into the boat, opened a hinged wooden box, and pulled out a long parcel wrapped in cloth.

"This is for you Robin."

"Whoopee! A telescope and a tripod," shouted the boy with delight when he had unwrapped his present.

"A quick lesson on how to use the mask, snorkel and fins - then I've got to go," said Mike.

Debra stepped down the steps into the sea. Mike was impressed by the way Debra immediately mastered the use of the equipment.

"You're a natural - a proper little dolphin," he said. He rummaged around in the inflatable and produced a belt with a single lead weight on it. He showed her how the quick-release buckle worked.

"This will make diving down easier. Ditch it if ever you feel tired and want more buoyancy," he said just before he sped off back to *Merlin*.

12 A new world

The fins, mask and snorkel opened-up a new world for Debra. She spent hours floating on the surface close to the rocks gazing into the fissures that cut into the cliff. She watched wriggly eels that sparkled like strips of tinsel. She gazed into gulleys and chased after shoals of little silver fish that fled in front of her. She hovered over sea urchins and starfishes.

Debra watched in wonder at a jelly fish. Its transparent dome was wreathed with strips of neon blue. It moved with rhythmic pulses, like an umbrella that opened and closed all by itself.

When the tide was right out she snorkelled down below the seaweeds. There she discovered banks of sea anemones as beautiful and colourful as any flowers that grew on the land.

She liked taking a deep breath and snorkelling through the long gulleys which were like underwater valleys. But more than absolutely anything else she loved having Dilo for company. He never frightened her again, always approaching very slowly, making sure she could see him before he got too close. Then he would swim quietly with her as she finned into the depths.

As time went by her confidence built up and so did Dilo's. Then one evening the magic happened. It was the result of an impulse. Debra, wearing just her swimming costume, decided to have one last swim before going back up to the lighthouse. She dived in from the rocks and pulled herself down deeper and deeper with powerful breast strokes. Suddenly she was aware that Dilo had joined her. She could see his blurred image moving excitedly around her. She had never seen him swim so fast underwater before. Debra stayed down for as long as she could. When she finally ran out of breath she headed quickly upwards.

As Debra split the surface there was an explosion beside her. Dilo fired himself out of the sea. For a moment she was aware of him flying over her with water cascading from his body. Then he nose-dived back into the sea with a glorious splash. Tingling with excitement Debra looked around wondering what he would do next. The waves subsided. Everything was quiet. The dolphin had disappeared. Or so she thought. She swam slowly ahead looking all around. Nothing. Then by chance she glanced down. Dilo was right underneath her, very close. He was coming up. Dilo was pushing her. Her speed increased.

Then, lifted from below, Debra rose out of the water, her legs astride the dolphin. She was sitting on Dilo and moving forward.

Debra raised her arms aloft. She was riding Dilo.

"Wheee," she cried as the dolphin carried her across the sea. Then her life went into slow motion.

Debra felt as if she was on a fairground carousel - gently rising and falling - riding a seahorse instead of a wooden one. The foam quietly swished round Dilo's head. Her legs pulled trails of white bubbles through the water. Rocking to the rhythm of the up and down movements of Dilo's tail she was travelling through a dreamworld. The sky was ablaze with tangerine light. On and on she journeyed across a sea scattered with sparkling orange-yellow stars.

In the distance the lighthouse stood boldly on top of the cliffs. Its lantern silhouetted against the flaming sky looked like the turret of a fairy-tale castle. Debra would not have been surprised if Dilo had turned into a unicorn, sprouted wings, and carried her aloft into the sky and the setting sun.

Debra's reverie stopped as quickly and surprisingly as it started. Suddenly Dilo dived. The girl was once again human, back in real time, in the real world, swimming in the wide open sea.

Debra looked up at the cliffs. Leaning on the wall watching were her brother, her uncle and Postie - who had come out for an evening stroll. She waved and they all waved back. Dilo was floating gently on the surface alongside her.

"Is that a reflection or a star on the dolphin's dorsal fin?" Postie asked his friend Pat.

"Debra's mentioned it several times," came the reply. "I couldn't see it at first, but now I can ."

"So can I ," added Robin. "Yesterday I saw it quite clearly through my telescope. A man on the cliff path asked if he could have a look at the dolphin. When I told him to look for the star he said he couldn't see it at all."

"How strange," added Postie.

"Perhaps he's a magic dolphin," said Pat with a grin.

"Many a true word is spoken in jest. One thing's for certain, he's a very special dolphin," commented Postie.

13 "Help"

The next morning Debra couldn't wait to get back into the water.

"I'm going to see if the dolphin will come and play with me again," she said to Robin. "Are you coming?"

"I'll stay and watch from up here," said their uncle as the two scrambled excitedly down the steps. Debra was in her wetsuit and carrying her fins, mask and snorkel.

"You should learn to swim Robin," said Debra.

"No thank you," he replied. "I'd rather stay on *terra firma*," which was exactly what he wasn't going to do for much longer.

Debra picked up two pebbles she kept on the steps. She knew that if she clapped them together Dilo would hear the sound wherever he was in the bay.

Debra sat on the bottom step and put on her fins. She pulled the mask into place and sucked through her nose to make sure it was a tight fit.

"See you later Robin," she said before biting onto her snorkel mouthpiece and launching herself into the sea.

Dilo barely heard the splash, but he did hear the crack of the stones. He immediately raced towards the source of the sound. The dolphin was underneath Debra and looking up at her before she had finned a short distance from the rocks.

"Hello dolphin!" she exclaimed through her snorkel tube.

Robin heard more distorted words coming from his sister's snorkel tube.

"That girl talks to that dolphin as if it was human," he said to himself, sitting on the steps watching Debra swimming in circles. Then he spotted a toy sailing boat that had been washed-up

85

onto the rocks.

"I wonder who has lost that?" he muttered to himself as he climbed on all fours towards it.

Above him his uncle was talking to a man who had been walking along the cliff-top path. The hiker enquired about the lighthouse. He said he was a journalist. He asked if he could take pictures of the lighthouseman with the lighthouse in the background. After he had finished the two men leaned on the wall and Debra's Uncle told him of her remarkable ride. The stranger was keenly interested. When he caught sight of Debra and the dolphin he took a video camera out of his back-pack and started to film. He zoomed-in on the floating figure of Debra. A moment later, through his viewfinder he saw her fins rise out of the water and then slide swiftly from view as the girl expertly dived into the depths.

Underwater Debra put her arms straight ahead and swam with legs together - the dolphin stroke. Dilo was alongside her, matching her movements. When she spiralled deeper the dolphin spiralled too. Down into a valley between the rocks she raced with Dilo in hot pursuit. Like a mermaid, with her long hair trailing in undulating waves, Debra flew past tall seaweeds. Looking up she saw the blue sky, white clouds and a brilliant sun shining like a disc in the silvery surface high above. She soared up towards it with the dolphin beside her.

Debra and Dilo breathed together as they surfaced - the sharp sounds of their breaths mingling. Without thinking Debra cupped her hands round Dilo's dorsal fin. The next minute

she was skimming across the water being towed by the dolphin. The water was swishing up between her arms and pouring over her shoulders. Her "Eeeks" of delight could be heard by onlookers on the top of the cliff.

Away from the land they raced. Debra could sense Dilo's tail pumping up and down beneath her. Her fins trailing through the water were leaving a wake of white foam. Faster and faster they sped. Holding on tight with arms outstretched, Debra could feel the pull on her shoulders.

Dilo carried Debra into the middle of the channel. Then quite suddenly he rolled. The dolphin's fin slipped from between her hands. Dilo submerged and Debra was left floating - breathless with excitement. She looked across at the cliffs. Her uncle was running down the steps as fast as he could.

The word "Help" came across the water. She saw an arm waving frantically.

"Help, Help." Then there was silence.

14 Rescue

When Robin slipped on the seaweed and fell into the sea he felt the water close over his head. He kicked madly with his feet. It seemed an age before he got his head above the surface again. He tried to breathe but water came into his mouth and he started to choke. He desperately tried to grab a rock but couldn't quite reach it and sank again. He was still choking when he managed to kick himself back to the surface. There was a slight current running. The safety of the rocks was moving away from him.

"Help, help!" he shouted, waving his arm in the air before sinking again.

"I'm going to die," he thought. The boy desperately wanted to breathe. But there was water all round him. His throat was in spasm. He couldn't hold out any more. He was losing consciousness. Then something soft was pushing him up. At first Robin was only partly aware that he was back on the surface, supported from below. He coughed out a mouthful of water. Then some urgent words came out of nowhere into his head.

"Hold on! Hold on!"

It was his uncle's voice

"Uncle Pat, what are you doing inside my head?" he asked himself in a semi-conscious state.

"Hold on! I'm . . . . " Robin didn't hear the rest of the sentence. He was swallowed in a green haze.

Debra heard the urgent message travel across the water.

"Hold on! I'm coming to get you."

She saw her uncle at the base of the cliffs. He was frantically pulling on the running line. Water was dripping from the tassels of seaweed hanging from it. His clinker rowing dinghy was moving towards the steps in rapid jerks.

In the distance she could see the grey curved dorsal fin of the dolphin. A red bundle was draped over Dilo's back. She recognised the colour. It was Robin's shirt. Her twin brother was laid across the back of the dolphin like a sack of potatoes, his arms hanging down in the water on one side, his legs dangling on the other. Debra started to fin as fast as she could towards the dolphin who was staying still. She heard Dilo breathe with a sharp loud puff.

The sudden noise awoke Robin. The world around him slowly came into focus. He could feel the firm round body of Dilo under his chest. His head was flopped to one side on his shoulder. He could see the dark grey shape of the dolphin with water alongside it. A small wave slapped into his face. Robin spluttered and raised his head. He was in a thick fog. Through the mist he could see his uncle pulling hard on the oars of the dinghy.

Suddenly his sister was beside him. She spat out the mouthpiece of her snorkel.

"Thank goodness you are alright," she blurted out.

"Stay there, don't move. Uncle Pat is coming."

Debra gently stroked Dilo's head. The dolphin slowly moved forward, still supporting Robin's limp body.

A few moments later the boat was alongside. His uncle expertly shipped the oars.

"Take it easy Robin. You're alright now," he said very reassuringly. "Give me your hand."

As he took hold of the boy's hand the dolphin slowly sank. Dilo surfaced again immediately beside Robin. Debra swam up behind her brother.

"Can you hold onto the gunwale?" said Uncle Pat, placing the boy's hands onto the side of his boat. "Gently does it. Easy now."

The boat was tilting over.

"I'll have to pull you in over the stern."

Robin was slowly manoeuvred to the back of the dinghy.

"One, two, three, up!"

A few moments later the boy was in the dinghy and his uncle was rowing him to the steps. Debra snorkelled behind, followed by Dilo.

15 In the news

The next day Postie came to the lighthouse. His arrival was announced by Boka who was barking loudly. The postman walked through the open door, straight into the kitchen. He threw a newspaper down onto the table.

"Have you seen this?" he said, with a note of triumph. The folded paper opened as it landed. Dominating the page was a photograph of Dilo with Robin across his back, Debra in the water and the dinghy alongside. Above it were the bold headlines: DRAMATIC RESCUE. Underneath in capitals was the caption DOLPHIN GIRL'S TWIN BROTHER SAVED BY DOLPHIN DILO.

Debra's eyes filled with tears when she saw the picture.

"Saw the whole thing on the telly last night," continued Postie.

"Who on earth filmed us?" said Robin.

"It must have been that man I was speaking to on the top of the cliff. He did ask a lot of questions. I told him all about you."

"I didn't know you'd given the dolphin a name," said the postman.

"Nor did I," said Debra. "I always called him Dolphin."

"I must have told him that was the code name Robin and I use when we put his details into the computer."

"What's this about you and computers Pat?" enquired Postie.

"Uncle Pat and I are putting all of the details about the dolphin on my computer aren't we?' said Robin looking at his uncle for confirmation. "Uncle Pat's getting really good at it."

"Computers indeed. Well there's a turn up for the books."

"Well we've all got to move with the times," piped up Robin.

Debra was worried that her uncle would be offended by her brother's remark. But he wasn't. The boy and his uncle had become even closer since the accident.

"That's right Robin. Try to anyway," the lighthouseman added with a wry smile.

"What letters have you got for us today Postie?" asked Debra, hoping there would be one for her.

"One each." The postman handed out the letters. "They're all in the same handwriting," he continued. "Looks like they're from your mother," he said to the twins.

The children opened theirs immediately.

"Well, what does she say?" asked their uncle, putting his unopened letter on the dresser.

Robin started first.

"Dear Robin, thank you for your letter. A computer print out is easier to read than your writing. Exclamation mark." Robin looked up with a grimace. "What a cheek," he exclaimed. "I am pleased that you have settled in well and that you are teaching your uncle to use your computer. Please remember that not everybody is as potty about computers as you are. I hope you are getting outdoors more. Have you learnt to swim yet? Must go now. Love Mum."

"The writing on mine is very wobbly," said Debra. "But here goes. Dear Debra. It sounds like you are having a lot of fun. How exciting to see a dolphin. I always wanted to but never have. Perhaps I will one day. Give your brother lots of hugs from me. Take care. Love Mum."

"It's very short," she added after a brief pause.

"Well I expect she is still very tired after her operation," said Robin.

"Will you stop for tea?' asked the lighthouseman looking at Postie.

"No thanks, I've got to get on my way. I thought you would want to see the paper, so I put you at the head of my round today."

"Will you post this for me please," said Robin handing him a letter.

The postman looked at the address.

"International Wildlife Watch," he said. "Of course I will young man." With that he stepped out into the bright sunshine.

The lighthouse keeper didn't open his letter until the children had gone to bed. When he saw

how uneven the writing was on the twins' letters
he had a feeling all was not well with their mother.
He was right.

Dear Pat,

Thank you so much for being so wonderful with Debra and Robin. Their letters are full of praise for you. They are obviously enjoying themselves;

I am sorry to tell you that the operation was not a success. I keep being sick. The consultant said he is going to try something else, but first I must get my strength up. Some hope. I'm very weak.

Sorry I can't write any more. I feel so tired. Tell the children I love them and miss them very much.

Your loving sister,

Mary.

16 Picnic on the cliffs

The news about Dilo spread like wildfire. The next weekend lots of people came to the bay. Many trailed up the path to the lighthouse. Some came with flasks and sandwiches. A whole group went swimming from the lighthouse steps calling out "Dilo, Dilo". When the dolphin swam among them there were shrieks of delight. Everyone seemed to have a camera. Lots of small craft came. On and off all day long boats buzzed out from the slipway in the harbour. Dilo didn't mind at all. In fact he seemed to like the extra attention.

The two fishermen who took visitors on round-the-bay trips did a roaring trade. They usually pointed out various features to their passengers. Now they had a new topic to add to their commentaries. With each trip they embellished their stories. By the end of the day they had it word perfect.

"On your left you will see the lighthouse." Then with an expansive gesture, "Over there is the very rock from which the boy fell. The treacherous current took him to the middle of the channel before the dolphin reached him."

At the beginning they said, "I expect you all saw it on television." But by the end of the day they found it better to pause for dramatic effect.

"Did any of you see it on television?" Of course most of them had. That's why they came. When a forest of arms shot up, the boatmen knew they had everyone's attention.

"Has anyone seen Dilo yet?" was their next question.

"No!" all the passengers roared.

"Then let's see if we can find him."

Usually within a few minutes of a boat arriving near the lighthouse, Dilo would appear.

"There he is!" someone would shout,

pointing in the direction of the dolphin's fin before it disappeared. The boatmen would then head in that direction.

If a boatman was lucky Dilo would pop up alongside. When this happened his passengers rushed to one side of the boat and leaned over. Everyone, from grandmas to young children, would shout with delight when they spotted Dilo. Many of the passengers hanging over the side would stretch out their arms and try to touch Dilo's fin as it passed by.

When Robin and Debra were asked to pose for photographs they realised how much they had come to enjoy the peace and quiet of their lighthouse life. They decided they didn't much like publicity. So they made up a picnic and headed for a depression on the top of the cliffs. There, hidden from the footpath, they had a view of the entire bay and the harbour.

After eating their food the twins lay on their backs on the soft spongy grass. The warm air smelt of wild flowers. Above, the sun shone in a sky of cornflower blue. Puffs of cloud drifted lazily by. The excited voices of the dolphin watchers on the boats came floating up to them and mingled with the cries of the gulls. The white triangular sail of a distant yacht slid slow as a snail across the sparkling sea towards the harbour.

The noise from an engine with a high speed whine broke their reverie. Out from the harbour mouth a craft was zooming . You couldn't call it a boat. It had handlebars - rather like a motorbike.

Sitting astride the saddle was a man wearing a fluorescent wetsuit of bright orange and vivid green.

"What a show-off," said Robin to his sister as the jet-ski headed towards the channel beneath them.

Dilo rushed across to it. The man started to zig-zag. The dolphin cut across the wake and jumped over the small waves. The driver continued his journey out past the lighthouse into the bay, with the dolphin rushing alongside. Dilo followed him far from the pleasure boats and the swimmers. The man stayed out in the bay on his jet-ski, zooming here and there with Dilo racing around him.

"How selfish can you get," said Debra indignantly. "He's spoiling it for everyone." She was getting angry. "He's shattered our peace and quiet and he's taken the dolphin away from all those people who've come to see him. I wish that awful man and his wretched machine would go somewhere else."

"It's a free country," said Robin.

"I don't care," said Debra. "Those things should be banned."

Eventually the jet-ski rider got tired of chasing around.

"Thank goodness he's going," said Debra as the man raced back to the harbour. When she saw him curve off towards the beach she erupted again.

"Look at that!" she exclaimed, "He just missed that swimmer. He's only gone in close so that everyone can see him."

"Show off!" she shouted towards him. Her words were lost in the noise of his engine.

The sun went down and the crowds dispersed. The twins walked slowly back to the lighthouse. Their arms and legs were aglow where the sun had been shining on them.

"I'm hungry," said Debra.

"You're always hungry," replied Robin. When he smelt the casserole cooking in the range

Robin felt hungry too. But he didn't say so to Debra. Instead, as they walked-in through the door he said, "Uncle Pat, that smells delicious."

17 Sea Wolf

That evening everyone, including Boka and Sprat, went outside to have one last look for Dilo.

"What's that?" asked Debra pointing towards a boat speeding towards the channel.

"Whatever it is it's going fast," said Uncle Pat. Robin kept his telescope on its tripod by the window in the bedroom. He went into the house and reappeared carrying it over his shoulder. He set the tripod up beside the wall.

"What a sinister looking boat," said Debra. "From here it looks all black."

Peering through the eyepiece of the telescope Robin brought the vessel into focus. He could see water thrust up in a huge vee from the bow. Through the flying spray he could just read the name.

"It's called *Sea Wolf*," he announced.

The boat passed through the channel beneath them into the wide spread of the main harbour. But it did not head for the jetty as expected. It curved round towards the rocks opposite.

"Hey look, Dilo's gone to investigate," shouted Debra when she saw the dolphin's fin surface in the wake.

"That's a hazardous place to take a boat in," said their uncle watching *Sea Wolf* as it nosed in towards the cliffs.

"There's a man on the bow," said Robin still looking through his telescope. "He's looking into the water and directing the helmsman."

The boat eased slowly into a channel bounded by steep rocks. Just before it disappeared from their view Robin said, "Another man has come on deck. He's carrying a parcel."

The trio watched and waited in the dimming light. Time went by,

"I wonder what they are doing in there?" said Debra eventually. Then she added, "Look, there's something moving on the cliffs."

Robin swung his telescope to get a better look. "There's a man scrambling up the rocks," he said. "I think it's the man who came out of the cabin." Robin paused. "Yes it is. He's still carrying the parcel."

"They must have put him ashore," said their uncle. "That's a dangerous place to climb up the cliffs. I wonder why they didn't take him to the jetty?"

A short time later the boat re-emerged from between the rocks travelling backwards.

"Is the dolphin still with them Robin?'

The boy adjusted his telescope.

"Yes he's right under the stern," replied Robin.

The engine sound rose sharply. At the same moment the boat spun round in its own length. It hesitated for a moment.

"She must have twin screws," said Uncle Pat. "You couldn't manoeuvre like that with only one propeller."

They all heard the thunderous roar of the two engines as the boat accelerated. It rose onto the plane and hurtled away from the rocks in clouds of flying spray. A few moments later it was heading through the channel and out to sea. They didn't see Dilo again.

By now it was quite dusk.

"He's got no navigation lights," commented

Uncle Pat.

The children and their uncle packed up and went back into the lighthouse cottage for the night. They talked happily, unaware that the water in the channel which *Sea Wolf* had just left was turning red with blood.

18 Twin propellers

Dilo enjoyed the day the tourists flocked to see him.

He quickly came to recognise the slow throb of the two boats that brought parties out into the bay. He liked to hear the children shrieking "Dilo, Dilo!" when he surfaced alongside. Their joyful shouts filled him with pleasure. He enjoyed seeing bare arms hanging over the side of a boat and the outstretched hands trying to touch him.

The arrival of a jet-ski added to the amusements of the day. The vibrations it sent through the water were different to other boats he had played with. There was no propeller he could sneak up to. Instead a stream emerged from its tail like water from a powerful hosepipe. This set up pressure waves he could sense with his body. One of the things he enjoyed about the jet-ski was that it could twist and turn, almost as quickly as he could, but only on the surface of the sea.

How different it was to the boat that moved almost silently across the water, pulled it seemed by a white sheet tied to a stick. He liked that too, for completely different reasons. Although exciting it was also gentle. The sailing boat fits in with the rhythms of the air and the sea the dolphin thought to himself.

Then, when the day was nearly finished and everything was getting quiet, he heard a new sound. A very loud sound. It was thundering across the bay. Dilo rushed out to see what it was. He had to swim fast to get close.

As Dilo approached from underneath he could see two propellers churning the water into foam. Their power was enormous. He didn't go close. Instead he rode one of the waves that streamed out diagonally from the stern. It was a wonderfully exhilarating ride that carried him through the channel to the cliffs. The engines suddenly slowed. Dilo moved in for a closer inspection. He watched the hull nose between the rocks, the propellers moving slowly. Then they stopped completely and the vessel floated forward with its own momentum. The thud of the two powerful engines inside the hull continued at a slow pace.

Dilo swam underneath right up to the front. A man with a boathook was leaning out. The dolphin surfaced just as the bow of the boat gently bumped against the rocks. He heard the man with the boathook shout, "Jump". Another man with a parcel under one arm leapt across the gap onto the rocks. As soon as he landed the crewman pushed off. Dilo was still under the bow. He heard the engine noise increase. The propellers, working in reverse, were thrusting water from the back of the boat towards him. This was another new sensation - water flowing under the hull instead of out from the stern. Dilo followed the boat as it steadily backed out of the channel. It was getting dark. Above him the low pointed bow was silhouetted against the deep blue sky. The hull was completely black. In small white letters were the words *Sea Wolf.*

As the *Sea Wolf* slipped gently backwards Dilo decided to investigate the propellers. He could feel the power of the engines throbbing above him as he swam under the hull. Closer and closer he went. Soon he was between the two propellers sensing a new pleasure - vibrations coming into both sides of his body. By now the *Sea Wolf* had backed well clear of the rocks. The helmsman decided to turn the boat round and head back to sea. It was at this point, swift as lightning, that disaster struck.

One propeller went at full speed in one direction. The other in reverse. The water around the dolphin suddenly boiled into a violent turmoil. The noise was tremendous. The vessel was turning in its own length. Dilo was thrown to one side. Before he could react he felt the blades of one of the propellers slash into his head. The instant this happened he twisted his body violently and the other propeller chopped into his tail like an axe. Dilo thrashed with all his might. He was clear in a second. The water was vibrating with a tremendous roar. The sea all around was being torn to shreds. He was in an underwater maelstrom. Bubbles were swirling and flying in all directions. The noise of the engines changed. One of the propellers slowed. At the same moment the other stopped. An instant later it started again but was spinning in the opposite direction. Both engines screamed into full power. *Sea Wolf* hurtled forwards. The backwash sent waves crashing onto the rocks. Amidst them, like a floating log was the dark grey shape of a dolphin. A red stain was spreading into the water around the body. The bubbles cleared. The sea calmed and the *Sea Wolf* disappeared.

Instinct told the semi-conscious dolphin he must stay on the surface. A puff of red spray flew into the air as he blew through his blowhole. Through the black and moonless night Dilo rocked, like a piece of flotsam, in the gentle swell. With the incoming tide he drifted slowly back into the channel between the rocks.

When dawn came Dilo listlessly moved his tail. The dolphin slid slowly forwards, past the place where the man went ashore. The channel widened and he found himself in a pool surrounded by high cliffs. The sound of his sharp breathing funnelled upwards and was lost in the sky overhead. He circled slowly. He needed peace. In the centre of the pool a small rock rose up from the seabed, producing a tiny island that was submerged at high tide. He moved alongside and closed the eye closest to the rock. There he hung motionless in the water. He switched off his senses. He did not hear Debra's stones banging together as she tried to call him with her own signal. He did not hear the sound of the engines of the pleasure boats that were looking for him. All he heard was the occasional squawk of a gull.

Dilo stayed alone in his sanctuary all day, unaware that Debra was out looking for him.

19 A ray of hope

The morning after she had watched the arrival and departure of *Sea Wolf* Debra went into the sea as usual. She dived down and clicked her stones expecting to see Dilo's smiling face appear through the blue-green water. But the dolphin didn't show up. Four times she went into the water throughout the day. After each swim she became more and more concerned.

"I can't think what has happened to Dilo," she said to Robin.

"I've been looking everywhere through my telescope," he replied. "I haven't seen a trace of him anywhere."

That evening they were all glum as they sat round the table eating the stew that had been simmering on the stove for most of the day.

"I've been watching the tripper boats and I've spoken to the fishermen," said Uncle Pat, "but none of them have seen Dilo. I hope nothing has happened to him."

"I expect he's gone off fishing somewhere," said Robin. "He'll probably be back tomorrow."

"I've got a feeling deep inside that something's wrong," said Debra.

"Well there's nothing we can do about it now," said her uncle. "Off to bed the two of you."

Before he climbed into bed Robin looked up at the stars through his telescope. He carefully locked the head on the top of the tripod and asked his sister to have a look.

"That constellation is called 'The Dolphin'," he told her.

On the other side of the channel in the open-topped cave, Dilo was feeling very lonely. He looked up into the sky. There in the heavens he saw his mother in the stars. For the first time since the accident he felt a warm ray of hope. Her spirit was around him. Slowly his loneliness disappeared.

20 R & R

The next morning before breakfast Robin, Debra and their uncle went outside and stood by the wall looking out. There was still no sign of the dolphin.

Debra looked across at the cliffs and gulleys on the opposite side of the channel.

"Uncle Pat," she said, "would you row us over to the place where the black boat put that man ashore?" Debra paused. "Please," she added pleadingly.

Her uncle thought for a moment.

"We'll go over when the tide slackens. It'll be easier then."

"Can I take my mask and fins?"

"I don't see why not."

"I'll stay behind and keep a lookout with my

telescope," declared Robin. His sister understood why he didn't want to go out in the boat.

After lunch Debra and her uncle descended the steps. The lighthouseman pulled in the dinghy using the running line. Debra tossed her fins into the boat.

"You sit at the stern," said her uncle, holding her hand as she stepped in. Then he pushed away from the steps and was soon rowing strongly across the channel. From her seat in the back Debra could see exactly where they were heading.

She pointed the way when they got close to the cliffs and directed her uncle into the fissure that *Sea Wolf* had entered. As they moved into the cleft, all sight of the lighthouse on the cliffs opposite disappeared. Soon it was too narrow to row. Debra's uncle pulled in the oars. He handed one to his niece.

"We'll have to paddle in from here," he said, sticking the blade of his oar straight down into the water.

Debra looked up at an arch of rocks that closed over their heads. Then she saw light. It wasn't a closed cave. It was like a huge rock bridge. They paddled on. The channel widened. The boat drifted into a large pool concealed inside the cliff. The water was absolutely still and pale green. Debra looked over the side.

"The water is wonderfully clear," she said, her voice echoing round the giant funnel that led up to the sky.

"I can see all the pebbles on the bottom. Look down there. I can see a fish."

But her uncle wasn't listening to her. He had heard a familiar sound.

"Shush!" he said urgently. "Be quiet for a moment."

They stayed silent, floating on the glassy pool. Then they both heard it.

"That's Dilo," whispered Debra, scarcely able to believe her ears. "That's Dilo."

They paddled slowly towards the rock in the middle of the pool.

There in the shade she saw the triangular shape of Dilo's dorsal fin. In a trice she put on her mask, fins and snorkel and slipped quietly into the water. Slowly she finned forwards towards the dolphin. Dilo stayed still waiting for her to come. He was pleased she had found him.

"Oh Dilo what has happened to you?" he heard her exclaim quietly through her snorkel tube. He felt her hand running soothingly over his head.

Debra looked down at the three deep cuts. They were starkly white. At the deepest parts of

125

the wounds she could see pale pink flesh. Tiny
wisps of blood were coming from them. There
was another white slash on his tail The dolphin
allowed her to continue stroking him. Then he
took a breath and sank. Debra watched his tail
pump slowly up and down as Dilo swam beneath

her in the still silent water. He disappeared under the thick kelp that was growing out from the black rock face.

The dolphin swam round the rock and surfaced beside the boat with a vigorous blow. Debra's uncle leaned over the side and stroked the gleaming wet dome of Dilo's head.

"You have been in the wars, haven't you" he said looking at the wounds. "Good job they missed your blowhole, or you'd have been a gonner."

"What are we going to do Uncle?" said Debra who was gently treading water beside the boat, her mask pushed up on her forehead.

"We'll leave him in peace and ask the vet."

Debra expertly pulled herself over the transom.

"Goodbye Dilo. I'll be back soon," she said as her uncle rowed back to the entrance. "I love you," she called over her shoulder as the dinghy glided underneath the rock arch.

When they were halfway across the channel one of the tripper boats came chugging towards them. A man with a television camera on his shoulder was filming the cliffs and the lighthouse. The boatman holding the tiller called across "We're looking for the dolphin."

"We've been looking too," shouted Debra's uncle in reply, pulling hard on the oars.

Later that afternoon Robin and Debra walked into town to the veterinary surgery. It was a long way and it was dusk when they returned.

"Well, what did he say?" asked their uncle as soon as the two youngsters stepped through the door.

"We told him exactly what we saw and said you thought he had been hit by a propeller."

"Debra even drew the shape of the wounds," interrupted Robin.

"He said dolphins often injure themselves in the wild," continued Debra.

Robin interrupted again. "He said they are a

bit like children always grazing themselves."

Debra continued. "Then he said their cuts usually heal up quickly without any problems, but deep ones leave scars."

"So what did he say we should do?" asked Uncle Pat.

"Nothing," retorted Robin, "but we should keep an eye on the dolphin and let the vet know if we see any signs of serious infection."

"If that happens," continued Robin, "we must call again and he will come out and have a look for himself."

"Actually," said Debra, "he said he would send his junior partner."

"That's right," said Robin. "He said he didn't fancy putting on a mask and snorkel himself. And I don't blame him."

"So it's R and R for Dilo," said Uncle Pat.

"What's R and R?" asked Debra.

"Rest and recuperation."

"I think we should go and see him twice a

day until he's better," said Debra.

"You can't take him grapes. Why don't you take him a tin of sardines?' added Robin who was feeling much happier since the veterinary surgeon convinced him that Dilo would get better. "I'm starving."

21 In peak condition

Dilo was thankful that he had found a place to rest but he didn't like being closed-in. Two days after the accident he ventured out into the sea. It felt so wonderful to be in the open water again he couldn't contain his joy. He hurled himself up into the sky in a glorious leap.

Robin, who was watching the cormorants standing on the rocks drying their wings, rushed into the house.

"Debra, Debra," he shouted. "Dilo's out. He's just done a huge jump."

Debra had never changed into her costume so quickly in all her life. She didn't trouble to put on her wetsuit, or gather her fins. She flew down the steps and dived into the sea. A few overarm strokes and the dolphin was alongside. She stroked him tenderly and then duck dived into the depths. Debra couldn't see clearly without her mask. She was surrounded by blurred images. There were fuzzy brown stalks of kelp with large broad dark leaves like table cloths. The sea was zircon blue. But more exhilarating than anything else was the grey shape of the dolphin winding around her.

Debra didn't have to see Dilo to know where he was. When he was behind her she could *feel* his presence. His spirit filled the water. The water wasn't cold. She was aglow with joy.

Debra could hold her breath for ever it seemed. She felt she *was* a dolphin. She didn't know how long she stayed in the sea. It didn't matter.

Eventually, like all humans, Debra had to go back to the land. She pulled herself out onto the steps. She waved goodbye to Dilo and started to climb. Halfway up she turned and looked back. The dolphin was escorting a small fishing boat leaving the harbour, apparently none the worse for his terrible accident.

She was out of breath when she got to the top. She reached the door of the lighthouse cottage just as the postman was leaving.

"Hello Postie," she said gasping.

"There's a letter for you. It's from your mother. Robin's got it. It's good news. I'm on my way. Cheerio."

"Goodbye Postie," said Debra. She rushed into the house to see what the good news was.

Robin had the letter in his hand.

"Postie says we've got some good news from Mum," she blurted out. "What does she say?"

"It's to both of us," said Robin waving the letter.

"Dearest Twins," he read. "How are you both? Behaving yourselves I hope. H'm! do we ever do anything else?" added Robin.

"Go on, go on," urged Debra.

"I am out of hospital. I am staying at a place called Primrose House. It's a sanatorium. Everyone here is very kind. The weather has been wonderful and I am getting better every day. The doctors say they can't believe how well I am doing."

"Oh isn't that wonderful Robin," interrupted his sister.

"In fact," continued Robin, "they say I shall be fit enough to go home in a few days. So as soon as the house is sorted out I will make arrangements with Uncle Pat for you both to come back home in time for school."

"School - Ug!" said Robin with a look of mock disgust.

"I like school," retorted Debra. "So do you really."

Robin continued reading the letter, "From the sound of things you've been having an exciting time. When you get back I shall look forward to hearing all of your adventures. With lots of love to you both, Mum. P.S. I can't wait to see you."

"I've got some good news too," said Uncle Pat with a big smile on his face. He carefully spread out his letter on the table.

"Here, read it." Robin and Debra peered at the typed page.

Dear Sir,

     I am pleased to inform you that we have been approached by International Wildlife Watch. We understand they need a warden in your area and are proposing to offer you the post. Furthermore they are prepared to provide a grant sufficient to renovate the lighthouse cottage to bring it up to Ministry standards.

     This letter is to inform you that the Board have carefully considered this proposal and are prepared to extend your tenancy indefinitely should you accept the post of warden.

Yours faithfully,

E. Henderson
Supervisor

"Whoopee!" shouted Robin. "You're going to accept of course Uncle Pat. You'd make a wonderful warden."

Debra's eyes were full of tears. She rushed over to her uncle and hugged him.

"Oh Uncle Pat," she sobbed, "I'm so happy."

Debra's uncle was slightly embarrassed by

her embrace.

"You had better go and put some warm clothes on before you catch your death," he replied when Debra let him go. "I want to send you back home in the peak of condition."

"I shall put that statement with all my other records on my computer," said Robin, smiling broadly at his uncle.

"Remember that Debbie," he shouted after his sister as she went off to change.

"In peak condition!"

THE END

Notes

Why I like stories about Dilo.

Name: *Age:*
Address:

Picture

Draw your own picture of Dilo

Name	*Age*

Address:

Request from the author

I would love to know what you think about my Dilo stories and maybe
what you think Dilo should do next. If you can get them photocopied
please send copies of your Notes and Picture pages to me.
Horace Dobbs, Watch Publishing, 10 Melton Road,
North Ferriby, East Yorkshire HU14 3ET. England.
Thank You.

Letters from

North Ferriby

August 1995

Dear Reader,

Dilo has been swimming around in my mind since about 1978. When he finally leapt into reality on 1st January 1994 I was pleased with the form he took. So too it seems were you. I received heaps of letters telling me how much you enjoyed my book *Dilo and the Call of the Deep* . Many of you wanted to know when you would be able to read the next volume about his adventurous life.

Well here it is - *Dilo Makes Friends*.

Of course this book is not all my own work. Firstly there was Sue at Redcliff Studios who sat at her computer and transferred my longhand scribble onto a floppy disc - in a form from which her colleagues could produce this book.

I am one of those people who is not very good at spelling. So before the book was finally printed several friends, including Bridget Bar (aged 10), Maurice Darnell, Robin Petch and Kris Simpson read it carefully to check for typographical errors and any spelling mistakes the computer had missed. I thank everyone involved for their individual contributions. Also my thanks go to Rico whose magic pen and paints have helped so much to bring Dilo to life.

But Rico and the Redcliff team haven't finished yet because Dilo is already en-route for more adventures. These start when treasure is discovered and continue when *Sea Wolf* returns to the bay.

I am already looking forward to seeing *Dilo and the Treasure Hunters* in print.

With wishes for

Happy Dolphin Days

Sincerely

the Author

North Ferriby
March 2005

It is ten years since Robin and Debra first appeared in print. One of the magic things authors can do is to stop time. And this is just what I did. Over the years I wrote more stories about the Terrible Twins without them getting much older. So you can find out what happens to them next in *Dilo and the Treasure Hunters* and *Dilo and the Witch of Black Rock.* You should be able to get these books from the library.

But Rico and I haven't stopped yet. We've recently compiled a new book, *Dilo in Lighthouse Bay*, which will be published later this year. Once again the twins and Dilo find themselves caught up in an exciting adventure.

In this latest book I reveal why Debra and Robin have been dubbed the "Terrible Twins". Indeed, one of their escapades with a penguin nearly puts a stop to them getting back to see their beloved Uncle Pat. When they do return to Lighthouse Bay Debra and Robin discover that many things are different. So too does Dilo when he comes across a huge rig drilling for oil. Debra fears that its presence will change the bay forever. When there is an explosion on the rig it seems that she is right. But is she? You'll have to read *Dilo in Lighthouse Bay* to find out.

Happy Reading

Sincerely

Horace

DOLPHIN SHOP

IDW is an independent organisation that needs funds to keep going. These come from membership subscriptions, donations and from sales from the IDW Mail Order Shop.

The Dolphin Shop carries a wide range of products from bookmarks, DVDs and dolphin pajama cases to limited editions of poster size prints. Go online to *www.idw.org* for the latest offers or contact IDW Secretary (T: 01482 645789) for a free copy of the latest colourful catalogue.

DILO DOME

Thanks to the efforts of IDW and others our knowledge and understanding of dolphins has grown enormously in recent years. One of the major breakthroughs has been the discovery that real dolphins, and make believe dolphins like Dilo, can have a positive effect on the human mind and can help children in many ways - including those with special needs.

For information on the Dilo Dome visit *www.idw.org* or contact
Jackie Connell T: 07908 617318
E: jackie.connell@ntlworld.com

THE
DILO DOME

is a small portable dome in which children can experience the healing power of dolphins and their imaginations are free to wander joyfully like free dolphins in the open sea.

Join NOW - you wont regret it

INTERNATIONAL DOLPHIN WATCH (IDW)

The non-profit organisation that helps dolphins and people.

Activities include:

DOLPHIN WATCHING
DOLPHIN CONSERVATION • EDUCATION • HEALING

Members of IDW become part of a big dolphin loving family in which every individual is important.

MAIL MEMBERSHIP

Members recieve through the post a package of dolphin goodies including a dolphin identification chart, a dolphin watching guide and newsletters about the many activities of IDW including campaigns to make the seas cleaner and healthier.

ONLINE MEMBERSHIP

Online members receive, via email, a password that lets them into the Members Only Enclosure on the IDW website where there are complete books that can be downloaded and up to date information on dolphin watching around the world, with late booking bargains.

Visit the IDW website (*www.idw.org*) for information or contact:-
The Secretary, International Dolphin Watch, 10 Melton Road, North Ferriby, East Yorkshire HU14 3ET. England.
T: 01482 645789 F: 01482 634914 E: idw@talk21.com

DOLPHIN WATCHING GUIDE

Places to go to see dolphins including British Isles, Bahamas, Hong Kong, Australia, Gibraltar and many others. This attractive booklet, filled with colour photographs, comes with every IDW membership, or it can be purchased separately.

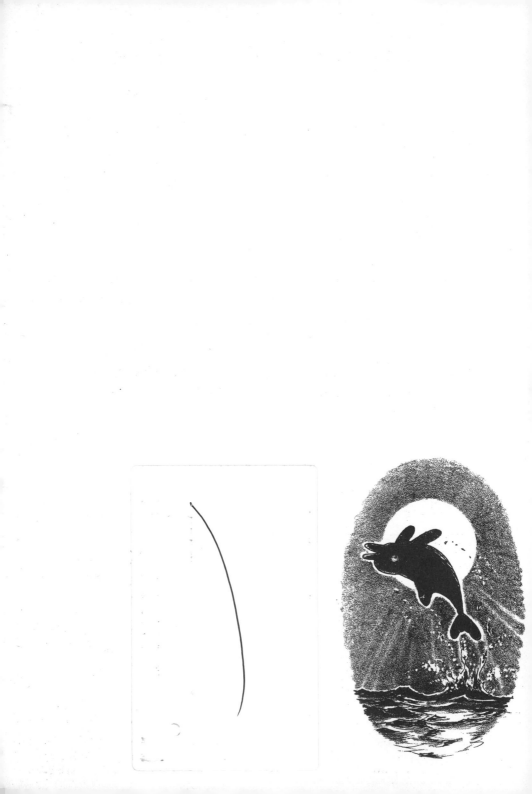